It is the year 2043… Warmer temperatures over time have caused landscapes to change… yet the earth and the people on it continue to survive and exist under the hot sun…

Prologue

The container stood prostrate and still as the scientist slowly made his way over to where it was. The afternoon sun shone down through the window of the room, the light reflecting on the metal from the outside of the container, the scientist having to shade his eyes momentarily. Taking a closer look he released the outer hinges to the box. Slowly grappling the edge of the surface of the container he gripped it and opened it, no sound coming from the lid at all…

He looked slowly at the face of the thing that stood inside; the object with its metallic lines, the intricacy of its design; the thing reflecting the shape of a human. It stood there cold and unused. The sun glared through the window as the scientist took a few more breaths, looking at what it was that stood before him; seemingly glued to it.

'Activate,' came the voice of the man at last as slowly the thing's eyes turned red.

Chapter One

For James the 9-5 grind had become increasingly difficult over the past couple of weeks. James was a dustbin man in the lower district of Arkansas, from *Sector 7* situated in the desert, mainly because room had become so scarce in the mainland cities. And so with what happens to most cases of overpopulation; *Sector 7* was formed, the splurging of buildings and infrastructure into the hot desert, making for the most part, *Sector 7*, an uncomfortable place to live. Allowed by the 'Arkansas' Agrarian' party who summoned the commission of the not so 'ecologically' town, '*Sector 7*' to be built, fairly soon distant warehouses started to appear from the desert ground up, high riser flats and supermarket complexes too, as well as clouds of great smog and carbon dioxide from factories, laboratories for work and research, and what seemed to be for more and more opportunities for industry.

'Built too quickly…' said some experts.
'A second rate place to live…' said others, there were some who believed the sector still had promise being so close to Yora, one of Arkansas' newer cities in the south. Yet despite all the talk, *Sector 7* was an industrial town nonetheless, quickly becoming full with new residents eager to work and find a moderately cheap place to live.
Yet despite the 'somewhat' interesting desert setting all around it, *Sector 7* remained on the bleaker side of locations… Silhouettes of buildings, factories and cranes in the evening allowing for the deep and somewhat non-inspiring terrain for the imagination… Maybe when the sand winds would pass through and the desert storms would kick up,

there would be a feeling of awe and belittlement about *Sector 7*, compared to the rest of the desert. But at the end of the day there was just sand, roads and factories to look at, and a lot of sand to clean up at the end of the sandstorms…

Yet - with employment rates up, it seemed the right choice for James at the time and so began his new life as a married couple in *Sector 7*, the location for the beginning of our story.

Not that James had particularly any reason to complain, for he had a steady job and a somewhat alright life with his newlywed - a writer for a charity magazine. Not pulling in the heaviest of income, yet still in love with her all the same, the two found the silver lining among the monotonous and hot days within *Sector 7*.

…However, strangely and circumvently James had had, not due to any reason of his own, become a little frustrated with life as of late… There were several reasons why, and these were the following.

The first reason was the adoption of his wife's new, one eyed cat Toby. Now Toby was no ordinary cat. He was a strong thoroughbred, a Manx breed in fact but with an arduous temperament to whine. Found from the streets by Lucy one Thursday evening on the way back from work, ardent to keep it, Toby unfortunately to the despair of James had been the constant cause of sleepless nights recently. (Lucy strangely enough was able to sleep through all of it) the cat often just sitting there in the midst of the one roomed studio flat through the early hours of the morning, whining endlessly, keeping all of James awake. James would eventually get up and send the cat a few scratches here and there, perhaps some milk and a few moments of attention - all of which seemed to never amount to anything.

The second reason was that not long ago James had hurt his back; he had torn muscle in his latissimus dorsi at work and had subsequently been flat on his back for a good week or so before returning to his job. Subsequently lifting or pulling anything had caused streaks of pain, but much to the dismay of James, his doctor had merely said, 'You're good to go,' after only what seemed a short duration of rest, hinting that his wound would heal 'in time,' and that 'it would be good not to expend his services (his job) whenever possible.'

The third and probably the most serious reason that had kept James close to his wits end recently was the fact that James was ultimately

to lose his work in the not so distant future...
Not immediately as of yet, but ever since the
last arrival of the .59 robotic wave sweeping
across Arkansas and the rest of America, it
wasn't only James that was found in the same
predicament. The .59 models were a part of
something becoming more and more frequent
by the day. Robots to look after the elderly, to
look after the young, to complete all the menial
jobs at work and sometimes even the more
complicated ones; robots to drive you to
school... It seemed like there was a never
ending supply, even the B2 bin lorry had
become semi-robotic in parts.

Alas James had been a dustbin man for the past
4 years of his life, yet as of only a few weeks
ago had been told by the firm that his position
would be under jeopardy, partially due to the
new .59 release from the United States Robotic
Corp. Soon enough there would be no need for
James or 'the boys' service.
The USRC was headed by David Mitchell, fast
becoming a household name in Arkansas and
abroad (the owner and creator of the USRC)
Eventually James was given a more accurate
dismissal period and upon hearing the final
news cursed to the highest extremities in receipt

of the letter by the dining room table that Saturday morning.

'Honey, is everything ok?' came the voice of Lucy, his newlywed turning when she heard his voice.

'Everything's… fine…' said James. But for James everything was not fine. Having followed the status quo for most of his life, not the type to go to university after falling short of the grades marginally, accepted the opportunity to work from a younger age, sealing his fate ungrudgingly to the slog of being a dustbin man. 4 years in with little or no promotion at all James had had in his mind reached a metaphorical dead end and with this latest news had promised himself to quite frankly, 'drop off it.'

'No, everythings fine honey,' said James, somewhat reassuringly again, hiding the letter under the rest of the bills and catalogs.

Chapter Two

The weeks passed as the duration of the days became longer, the sun beginning to stay higher in the sky.

The sound of the B2 bus woke James from the outside and with what little sleep he hadn't had, had become deprived even more. Toby was in his usual position near the kitchen sitting there mischievously ready to pur or start whining when he felt like it.

'You ready James?' came the voice from outside the window, the sound of the B2 bus' engine whirring and ticking as James groaned and yawned, the morning sun peering through, close to where their bed sat. Grumpily James stretched and sat up fumbling for the hook to open the window. 'I'll be there in 2,' came the disheveled voice. Hubert, his work colleague, was in the driver's seat of the B2, Mark, another of James' colleagues sitting next to him. Lucy as usual groaned and turned in bed, but with no need to get up and go just yet stretched in her covers and watched as James quickly got up, zipped on his jumpsuit, tended to his hair and teeth and in silence when all was done quietly closed the door behind him.

Yora, now like a metal metropolitan, coarse and brutish, massive and yet strangely unimpressive; was surrounded by 6 districts, the city center plus the 6 regions north, south, east and west of it. James lived in the south, *Sector 7*, whereby much of the sector was involved in food production and research, yet still close to the city center James had fairly quick access to the metropolitan as well as the other remaining sectors.

The skyscrapers toiled up from the city center in the distance providing shade for some of the city goers. Soon enough James could be seen shutting the door behind him on the ground floor which led to their one studio flat upstairs. Next to his flat was a Chinese takeaway restaurant and behind them there was even an outdoor metro that passed their flat shaking the surrounding buildings until late at night as the last of the trains winded their way downtown.

'Alright I'm coming,' shouted Dave from the door as he made his way to the van, bagel in hand.

'I'll see you later,' called his wife from up top. James jumped into the side of the lorry where there was one seat available, Mark and Hubert already in the front. 'You're gonna make us late,' said Hubert as he ran the ignition.

The city of *Sector 7* glistened in the morning sun as the B2 bus chugged along the streets for the beginning of its round. The bus zipped past those already walking outside to and about the sector, the strange silhouette of a robot holding the arm of an elderley lady as they drove past, another robot running alongside a human out for an early jog. The bus continued to drive through the town until it came to the edge of *Sector 7* between them and the city center, the three instinctually hopping out as they ran to each and every house aligning each bin onto the bin tipper at the back of the B2 bus.

The bus continued to drive through *Sector 7* as they passed each and every house on route, the sun passing high in the sky as the morning and early afternoon came and went.

Chapter Three

James stepped into the warm bowling alley from the cold night air, the sound of laughter, talk and music to be heard as he made his way over to the table where his friends Hubert, Mark and two other men were. Often the men would come to the bowling alley at least once a week to let off some steam, practice for their local team and hang out and be distracted from their everyday lives.

'What I can't stand is how much the USRC will be making from all of this,' said Hubert, mid-conversation, almost comically, shaking his head again as he stopped to take a drink of his beer.

'What you need is to concentrate on your score,' joked Mark as he in turn took a large chug of his drink.

The others laughed as Hubert in his second attempt nearly cleared all the bowling pins from the alley, minus two.

The evening passed with as much enjoyment as there could be within the short time, the clock ticking with the inevitable awaiting them, the sharp cold night air and the car ride home.

The bowling alley was a good respite for them, and particularly for James who enjoyed playing and competing when he could, the whole process taking his mind off things.

Chapter Four

It was a typical Thursday night and James had almost forgotten about the cat as he made his way into the flat amidst downtown sector 7, the last of the trains passing by as he silently opened the door, Toby already in his position as his wife Lucy sat sitting on the couch watching one of the late-night comedy shows on TV.

'How was the time with the boys?' said Lucy as she continued to watch the television, the flashing images beating against her face.

'Good,' said James walking over to the sink to get himself a glass of water, the floorboards creaking as his mouth made contact with the nice, fresh taste of water from the tap.

'Did you beat your personal best?' came the voice of Lucy taking an interest in James, turning to face James from the couch.

'Honey, is there something wrong…?' said Lucy finally, as she flicked and flicked through the channels nonchalantly; quietly, James saying nothing, as slowly he made his way over next to Lucy.

'I can tell when something's up you know... you just-   I guess it was the other day when you-…' and then she paused, facing the screen.

Slowly James took off his shoes and slid into the sofa next to her. 'Everything's fine,' he said lightly as he swung his arm over her shoulder.

'I just want you to be happy,' said Lucy again, quietly, under her breath. Not one to tell much of how he felt James kept quiet as the sound of laughing and cheering came from the television screen.

'Well, good' whispered Lucy finally.

'And how are the boys?' she said, as she turned to face James, reflecting, looking James keenly in the eye.

'Fine,' said James as he turned to the screen, turning to face Lucy, the sound of laughter once more in the background, 'Just fine.'

That night the cat whined, James sitting up much to the grief of his back. Slowly he got up and walked over to the cat who continued to whine, whining some more as James tried to pet him, the cat bearing reproach as he dabbed at James' hand, his claws partially out.

'What is wrong with you?' muttered James under his breath as he shook his head. 'Do we need to take you to the VET?' he whispered. James stood there momentarily, contemplating the cat and his own insomnia. Slowly he made his way to the kitchen, positioned at the far corner of the one roomed studio apartment turning the knobs of the sink to let out another cold swash of water. Silently he looked at his wife Lucy who was fast asleep and this made him jealous. Quietly, he made his way to the couch in front of the TV and took a seat as he flicked on the television, quickly lowering the volume so as not to wake Lucy. He watched aimlessly at the programmes as he flicked past each one until at last, something caught his attention. Sighing and seeing the inevitable, the lowered volume of the television ringing from its speakers, he saw the advertisement for the .59 series of robots displayed across the screen.

'Don't have time to finish the housework?' said the voice of the salesman '... or maybe you just need a friend? Well look no further…' came the voice of the man pitching the sale from behind the screen.

Another day came and James found himself already wide awake from Toby. Reluctantly he got out of bed as he prepared himself for the day ahead, the sound of the B2 rolling down the street.

'Another day, another dollar,' said Hubert as James jumped into the van, the fresh voice of Hubert momentarily giving a lift to James' day.

It was hot and sweaty outside and James soon found himself not wanting to be cramped in the hot B2 van as he tossed the bins back from the van to where they came from. Slowly the B2 bus made its way through its route, house to house, as James continued his work, the relentless sun beating down as he dragged each bin repetitively to the B2 and back.

Chapter Five

Slowly the days passed as the inevitable came, James feeling strangely more and more withdrawn with approximately a week or so to go until he would lose his job. It was 2am in the morning that night and the cat had kept him up again. He looked with jealousy at his wife as she slept calmly, not flinching an eyelid.

—

Yet again the cat continued to whine the following night. But for some strange reason it was almost as if it was quieter than normal, yet as if being awake was the last straw for James - he quietly made his way to the door of the flat, closing it behind him he descended the steps of his appartement and shutting the door behind him made his way outside. The fresh cold night air hit him almost making him feel better momentarily; the streets quieter at 2am.

Except leading towards the downtown gradually became a different story. Sirens were blaring in the night air, music playing from clubs, the convenience stores still open and the skyscrapers becoming more numerous, as they stood still like large figures planted within the dark of the evening. Normally James was not the person to go downtown much, but considering all that was amounting to at the time, tonight was a different story...

Quietly he made his way to a bar under an open roof positioned close to one of the skyscrapers, many different types of shops within James' proximity, some legal, others not so much.

He was greeted at the bar by a T-Robot Bartender.

'What would you like today, sir?' said the robot politely, the small sound of whirring as he moved his limbs, wiping down a couple of glasses held in hand with a towel. Reluctantly James scanned the beverages lined up in the back wall of the bar.

Neon lights from around the different shops shone through the night as James took the last couple of sips of his drink - strong enough to give him some kick, weak enough not to leave him particularly affected by the alcohol. There were two or three others at the bar, but strangely they kept themselves to themselves as the robot served each one quietly. Slowly James walked away from his seat and it was as if a sudden rush of blood ran to his head. He stopped, to contain himself, and began to wonder what it was that he had chosen to drink after all. Gaining his whereabouts once more he made his way under a small bridge that led out to a smaller road.

Strangely hearing muffled dance music in the background James, somewhat curious by the strange sounds made his way towards where it came from, strange lights about the place which eventually he found to be the source of the music. There were lights flashing from the window pane of the building; the entrance looking like a shop, a few people coming in and out of the building. And as if everything that had affected James; the inability to sleep, the harsh reality of his job ending and the irritance of everything that had had a hold on him there and that moment; James made his way over to the shop.

Not saying a word to the man who greeted him at the entrance, he   passed him, the man appearing to be watching, James walking through the ground floor rooms into smaller, darker rooms downstairs, the music blaring and becoming ever increasingly louder, the lights flashing everywhere. At first James didn't know where he was as there were about 3 other people in the room, chairs aligned in the pattern of a small, strange cinema with a large screen at the back of the room. Strange music blared out with different patterns of light and colors dancing this way and that against the walls. The must was almost unbearably loud, the strange rhythms and screeching of the beats as reluctantly James went and found a seat. Slowly he reached for the bag of substance in his pocket given by one of the members he had passed within the interior of the building. James took a seat.

Chapter Six

'Activate,' came the cheery voices of a number of people as the sound of cheering and applause came from that very house on the road. It was a hot summer's day and there seemed to be a party going on at 17 Banks Drive. It was the kind that suggested the family were expecting a new addition to the household, like a new pet or a child.

'Just think,' came the voice of the wife, 'I'll never have to do the dishes again.'
'And I'll never have to wash the car,' laughed the husband.

-

For James and the rest of *Sector 7* it was a new day as the sun came up once more, James finally back at his apartment tirefully staring at the ceiling of his apartment flat, the cat not long stopped whining, just as the sun had come up into the sky. Jealously he felt his wife asleep in the bed, her soft body warm next to his. Slowly he got up, James having woken up 30 minutes earlier than when his colleagues were due to drive by. Quietly he climbed out of his bed so as not to wake his wife, slowly he made his way to shower.

The cold water pricked at his skin as he drearily woke from his sluggishness, the quick and strange sensation of the cold water trickling down his body as he stayed put within the cold water, the realization dawning on him slowly that today was his last day at work. Quietly he dried himself and put on his usual jumpsuit ready for his last shift. Turning he faced his wife who was still sleeping not woken yet by his morning routine. Realizing he had forgotten something, he made his way to the dining table behind the couch and picked up a bag of powder. He stuffed it in his pocket, not wanting his wife to see it, he closed the door behind him.

'You're ready?' came the voice of Hubert in the driver's seat, as Mark opened the door for James to jump inside.

'Well folks,' came the sarcastic voice of Hubert at long last as the B2 bus drove through *Sector 7*, 'Today is the day.'

Slowly the men jumped out of their van as they began to run to each and every house to empty the bins. It was then that James saw the sight of a robot walking a dog the distance, James double-taking as he squinted in the sun, watching the robot nonchalantly walking the terrier down the road.

'Alright folks,' came the voice of Hubert as the day finally came to a close. 'Guess I'll be seeing you at the bowling alley,' James making his way out of the van.

That evening before bowling James had had other plans. Not wanting to tell Lucy where he was going he quietly slipped out of his appartement leaving Lucy watching the television once more. Turning off his phone he walked downtown, fumbling for the package in his pocket, checking it was still there. The night air felt good as he continued his way to where he had been a few nights back, but not stopping for a drink he walked directly towards where the music was playing, his destination. Rain started to pour, the rain quickly escalating as suddenly James momentarily distracted by luminous light in the corner of his eye looked to his left to see a bright billboard, shining brightly in the night air. Still with viable sound came noise from the board, the rain continued to pour. It showed David Mitchell from the USRC.

Begrudgingly James stopped and watched the man on the advert - David Mitchell smiling, looking relaxed and content in his suit as gradually he began to speak. And almost as if he was talking directly to James there and then he spoke...

'Wanting more in life?' said David, smiling. 'Just need that extra break or boost? ... Well I'm here to help ... I'll grant you one wish! That's right you heard me, you can ask me anything! To find out more, locate my scratch card and with the correct number on it, soon you'll be face to face with your dreams! ... See you soon.'

'What was that supposed to mean?' wondered James as the rain started to pour. James shrugged then headed over to where the music was playing from the middle of the street. Yet strangely enough as he walked through the main door towards the source of the music, the strange advert's image stayed in his mind. David Mitchell was smiling, like he was hiding something, or perhaps he was wanting the opposite, to share something special with somebody. 'Who knows!?' thought James. But eventually, too distracted by what he set out to do James walked through the different rooms and found the strange cinema again, reaching for another small bag of powder from his pocket, he sat back.

The following morning James, feeling the hard surface below him, found himself lying on a bench outside. He had been outside most of the night and had managed to sleep. Toby, nowhere to be seen. Slowly he opened his eyes as he heard the sound of a train passing by, the different sounds of early morning downtown in his ear, no music playing, just the eventual passing of cars and horns and activity as James got up and looked around him.

He had found himself in a small park downtown, the cooing sound of pigeons nearby as an older homeless man fed them close to where he lay. Almost like he was still wired for work, his body clock quickened… the eventual realization that today was his first day of unemployment, he sat up. His head hurt as he tried to fumble for a package in his pocket, finding nothing. Quietly he stood up, a gravitating ache in his head as gradually he came to his whereabouts, the sun beginning to beat down as he reached for his phone. 4 missed calls. All from Lucy.

James felt the inevitable coming as he staggered and made his way across the park, back to *Sector 7*, south from downtown.

'Where were you?' came the voice of Lucy as she opened the front door to their appartement. 'I called the police this morning you know. I had to-'

James, not answering, made his way to the sink and began to pour himself some cool water.

Chapter Seven

James made his way to the grocery store, the trip considered a 'punishment' by Lucy for not telling her where he had been last night. By the time he had had enough time looking at cereal boxes, vegetables, rice and everything else that you might need on a grocery visit, James made his way to the checkout holding his basket as he stepped forward in line, the checkout lady welcoming him. 'Good day,' she said. James smiled back; yet something strange caught James' eye as he stood there packing some of the food into his bag, his eyes spotting something at the back of the till. He saw what looked to be lottery tickets among the cigarettes and gum. It was a glimpse in the corner of his eye, had he not seen it he would have carried on packing, yet there was David Mitchell advertised at the back of the till, a lump of his 'business cards' piled down with what looked to be his face on it.

'How much are one of those?' enquired James, pointing to the cards.

'Oh they're free,' said the lady, 'Would you like one? You only get one though, mind you.' Slowly he reached out and took the lottery scratchcard from the lady. Thanking her he left.

-

The robot stood cold in the night air. Through all the fun and games the family that had bought the robot had forgotten to deactivate it. Back in its container yet still locked, the robot opened its eyes, the silence of the room, its eyes turning red. Like the robot had been born for the first time, it closed and opened its eyes once more, scanning what was around it, the side chair, the dining room table, the television, the couch. Feeling the walls of the container quietly the robot knocked on the frame of the box. The robot knew then instantly he was trapped inside, yet instead of calling for help he waited patiently around him, taking in his surroundings, it being the early hours of the morning, the early light of the dawn glowing from around the curtains. Quietly the robot knocked again, and then again but no one could hear him, the family still evidently asleep.

As the sun rose in the sky the sound of laughter could be heard at 17 Banks Drive, two girls, Angela, 7, and Kasey, 11, already up playing in their room as the parents slept on, Angela the younger of the two was role-playing with two dolls in hand whilst Kasey her sister sang to herself reaching for the coloring book that she had been working on the past few days. And almost forgetting about the arrival of the robot, Angela, running through the house and into the living room, suddenly stopped and looked at the container that stood before her. Slowly she took small steps as she made her way over to where it was looking at the robot through the see-through panes. Eventually she walked right up to it and within a few moments knocked on the window pane of the container, staring at what was inside, trying to make of it what she could. It happened then... the girl unable to keep her eyes off it, face to face and almost deceptively quick the robot opened his eyes, his eyes turning red, the flinch instinctually scaring the young girl causing her to scream and fall back. Within moments the parents and Kasey ran into the room.

'What happened, Angelica?' said the mother, turning to face her young daughter, the daughter holding her hands to her face crying recklessly as she pointed to the robot inside the container.

'It- it-' came the stammering of the frightened girl as she shielded her gaze from the thing.

'It moved,' came the voice of the girl still pointing to it as the father came over to her and assured her, giving her a hug.

'Now listen,' said the father, Kasey watching on.

'Be assured,' said the father, 'this thing won't hurt you... Watch,' said the father.

'Deactivate,' came the voice of the man, the robot standing frozen, nothing changing, its eyes no longer red, it appearing to be lifeless.

That afternoon the children were introduced to the robot more formally, the father saying 'activate' once more to turn the robot on. Slowly the robot's eyes blinked, then blinked some more as gradually his eyes glowed red, the red dissolving into a less intense color as gradually, like the robot had woken from some slumber, his whereabouts coming to him, smiled, then looked about him.

'I'm sorry-' said the robot finally, 'Do I?'

'Oh,' said the robot, 'You must be…'

'I see,' said the robot.

The family stood there opposite, smiling as they stood fixated and in awe, the robot moving, stretching out his arms and hands looking at his own hands and limbs.

'What's your name?' came the voice of Angela sweetly, feeling better.
'My name is L-300,' said the robot kindly, 'But you can call me Led.'

-

'Honey you forgot the milk,' called Lucy, coming from the kitchen of their one roomed apartment. James was showering in the bathroom. A couple of minutes later James came over, Lucy standing there. 'You forgot the milk,' said Lucy, her arms wide open in amazement that he had forgotten such an important thing.

'Honey; I'm sorry,' said James.

'No, no... ' said Lucy, her arms in the air, looking like she had had a bad day. James made his way over to her and began to hug her, trying to comfort her somewhat, his hand running through her hair. 'It was a mistake,' said James, smiling, as he continued to hold her.

'James...' said Lucy all of a sudden... 'Why aren't you at work?'

—

The next few hours James tried to explain everything to Lucy, why he had tried to hide it from her all this time. But Lucy didn't seem to take much in, it seemed she had had enough of just about everything there and then and in one impulsive move left the flat, leaving James on his own.

James sat there, aimlessly watching the television as the programmes passed by, he sat there watching a strange cooking show, not particularly caring. Finally picking up the TV remote once more he started to switch channels until, suddenly, at last, and as if by fate, it appeared once more - the exact same advertisement he had seen last night on the billboard downtown. It was David Mitchel, head of USRC standing there wearing a suit smiling on the screen, giving the same explanation about the strange 'lottery-type competition' he had set up and broadcasted all over town and beyond. Quickly it reminded James that he still had the card in his possession - but not particularly caring, slowly James got up and made his way to the dining room table. Fumbling around one of the plastic grocery bags he felt inside, feeling for the small card in his fingertips.

And so James rang the number on the card but instead of calmly waiting, all the anger that had pent up in him recently meant that for the person who picked up the call on the other end had to receive James' strange and sudden onslaught of emotion; about USCR, his job, David Mitchell, and everything.

'I'm sorry sir,' said the lady on the other line, 'But I will have to hang up if your tone like that continues...'

'But you don't care...' screeched James, 'What am I supposed to do now that all of your robots have taken our jobs!'

The lady hung up.

James stood there momentarily, then rang the number again.

'I'm sorry,' he said, 'I don't know what came over me. What I really meant to say was that... was that I really wanted to enter your competition...'

'Sir, do you have the card or not?' came the voice of another girl's voice.

'Oh, you're someone else...' said James.

'Well what's the number?'

Well,' said James clearing his throat, and saying sarcastically, 'Well there's an 8 and a 5 and a 2 and a 3 and a 7 and a 1 …'

There was a strange fumbling on the phone.

'Sir that's the winning number,' said the girl on the other line.

'Oh great,' said James, 'Not only have you taken my job, now I have to put up with some strange hoax, or that's it, a mass con.'

'No sir…,' said the lady on the phone, almost unbelieving, 'that's the winning number,' said the girl unmistakably. 'You're our winner sir.'

Chapter Eight

Persuading Lucy about what had just happened proved difficult for James.

'Sorry you've won what?' said Lucy, over the phone.

'The lottery... well, kind of the lottery. More like a wish...'

'A wish...?' said Lucy, confused.

'Yes, well an evening with David Mitchell.'

'An evening with David Mitchell?' said Lucy suddenly, 'And you expect me to believe that?'
'Well, I don't know exactly...'
'Well that's just great James...' said Lucy after a long pause. Then she hung up.

The long walk through downtown towards the northern side of the city center proved longer than James had expected. In just a shirt and jeans he trudged through downtown, the evening air strangely more hot and sticky than ever before. He passed through the roads noticing the bins put back perfectly into place and strangely he missed his job... despite all the large waste bins and junk he had to deal with, he missed it.

'25 Lexus street' was the address the lady gave over the phone, and so James made his way to the address using the GPS on his watch he found its location, a skyscraper, probably the tallest in Yora.

Upon entering the building it appeared to be almost empty with one lady at the back of the large hallway at a reception desk. 'I'm here to see David Mitchell,' said James, scouring the strangely eerie place. 'What's your name sir?' said the lady at the reception.

'James. James McCreary.'

'Take the lift to floor 52 and he'll be in room A, James,' said the lady.

It was no surprise to James that 52 was in fact the top of the skyscraper. No one to accompany him, the small lift swiftly escalated all the way to the top floor, no one around as it opened, a corridor of rooms down the left hand side and to the right. James turned right, and began to look for room A. With no one to assist him he scoured the different doors finding that room A wasn't until the far end of the corridor. Knocking but hearing nothing he waited a whole few seconds outside before slowly he opened the door.

-

The family looked proud as they walked with their new robot through the parks of Yora. Robots were getting more expensive these days and with what little money the family had had gone to the robot, the robot like a new car or an expensive accessory to show off, the father smiling as the robot walked with the two girls up front.

'I'm sorry,' said the robot as it watched the little girl Angela run ahead. Kasey was walking side by side with him. 'But I don't think I caught your names?'

'I'm Kasey,' said Kasey, 'And that's Angela.'

'Angela,' repeated the robot, like he had never heard the name before, watching as the girl skipped along in front.

Quickly the family made sure the robot felt at home and was included during dinner times, when watching television and so on. The robot was always there ready to do the menial jobs. Quickly the robot got used to life with the family and soon enough both Angela and Kasey had found themselves accompanied by Led to school, to dance classes and more of the like. Infact Led proved to be a lot more useful in these types of situations than first expected.

It was a hot summer's day when it happened… the morning routine just like any other as the robot woke the two girls, the parents still in bed. 'Morning Angela,' came the sound of the robot as Angela slowly opened her eyes. Quietly the young girl yawned and stretched as she saw the robot looking over her.

'Morning Led, ' said Kasey hearing the voice of the robot.

'Time for school, ' said the robot, kindly as he helped the girls up, helping them change their clothes.

'Morning Led,' came the voice of the father as the two girls sat contently with their cereal at breakfast in the dining room.

'And what do we have for school today?' said the dad.

There was a slight pause as the girls continued to eat their breakfast. Gradually Led butted in with all the information the father needed. 'Well for Kasey,' said the robot, 'Her day consists of math and reading in the morning, sport and history in the afternoon.' And for Angela, 'Drawing and mathematics- You had decided you were going to draw a butterfly for this morning's art lesson didn't you Angela, if I recall?'

'Uhuh,' came the voice of the girl as she looked at her father.

'That's great,' whispered the father, smiling.

The walk to school went as planned. Led holding the hands of both Angela and Kasey as they made their way from the north district, *Sector 3* to the edge of downtown, their school just between the inner city and the residential areas of the north. The morning was as warm as any other, the streets becoming busier and busier the further in they walked.

It was not as if this was the first time this had ever happened with a young girl like Angela, but if it wasn't for the robot she probably would have lost her life or something similar with the same severity. It was at the crosslights, Angela skipping along as normal, holding onto the hand of Led, Kasey holding the other, Angela tugging and pulling on Led who seemed to manage the both of them well. It was when they stopped at the crossroads that it happened, very quickly and enough to make the hairs rise on the end of your back, within a bat of an eyelid and enough to make Kasey cry, they stopped at a red light, but without a view of cars to the right, impulsively little Angela stepped out onto the road. Much to the horror of just about everyone there at the crossroads one car sped around the corner towards the crossing where Led and the two girls were. Just at that moment that Angela put her foot across the road, the car sped along coming out of nowhere and with little or no time to brake, if it hadn't been for the robot who quickly gripped the hand of Angela, Angela would have been hit by the car. Kasey screamed as in flash, with great power Led pulled the girl back, the car whizzing by - Angela practically pulled to the ground by Led. It took a few moments before Angela came to her senses, but when she did she began to cry… That day Angela was taken to the hospital for dislocating her arm and at first, enquiries were put in against the behavior of the robot. But if it hadn't been for Kasey, who told the school officials, the doctors, that Led had in fact saved her life, it could have been the end for Led.

'A car traveling at 50 mph obstructing a girl would most certainly result in fatality,' repeated the robot numerous times. The enquiry was investigated more and more until it turned out that Kasey was right, the robot had in fact saved Angela's life.

—

James entered through the door of room A immediately noticing the size of the room he had just walked into. Like nothing he had expected it to be, he stopped momentarily taking in his surroundings. Right in-front of him and all around him was light, brighter but more delicate than that of the evening air outside, artificial light shining down exhibiting different collections of plants and foliage through glass walls. Exotic ones that looked to be from every corner of the jungle, he walked through taking in his surroundings, wondering if he was in some sort of scientific exhibit or a science lab. Half distracted by the great plants and exotic foliage around him he made his way through the different rows of glass exhibits, almost forgetting about David Mitchell and everything that had happened prior, until within a flash he noticed movement from the other side of the room further back through the glass walls. Quietly James sped up and made his way round the exhibits until at last he saw a man on the balcony outside, a sheer glass doorway to the balcony which kept everything, the plants inside. Quietly James slid open the glass door that led to the balcony. They were high up, as James saw what looked to be Mr. Mitchell standing there looking out into the whole of *Sectors 6 & 7* to the south, his back to James. Almost as if James didn't want to interrupt the man, he too looked out and saw the sprawl of buildings and factories and residential houses lay flat across the desert. And almost as if James had suddenly become shy, or too embarrassed to speak, he said.

'Excuse me... Excuse me!' he said, a little louder, the man turning.

Chapter Nine

There were loud cheers as quietly little Angela tugged at the last of the ribbon that held firm the lid of the cardboard box to the rest of it. 'What's inside?' teased the mother as Kasey looked on in excitement, Angela pulling hard as somehow she managed to unravel the last of the ribbon bow. It wasn't long before she found out just what was in the box as she opened the lid, an excited sniffing and panting could be heard.

Led looked on in excitement as slowly shouts and cheers came from all parts of the family as what appeared to be a very excited dog scooped up in the arms of Angela, Angela who seemed almost too emotional to care. 'We'll call it Bess,' said the girl's mum as the two quickly made friends with the little dog.

Led looked on and smiled. He noticed the contentment of the family, the glisten in their eyes as they saw the living thing enthralled, embraced by the cheers and the hugs of the two girls and the parents. 'How could it all be so nice, so complete,' half-wondered the robot as he looked on. But nonetheless he knew in his mind that they were all happy and content, and that their safety was intact and perhaps that's all that mattered, thought the robot.

—

'Excuse me sir.'

David Mitchell turned and looked at the man as the red evening sky shone down on the skyscraper and the rest of the sectors. The man looked to be in some sort of meditation as finally he turned and looked at James standing before him.

'Well, you must be the winner,' he said.

'Yes, yes I am'

The evening sky was like a hot orange as the light reflected on the desert spanning out in all directions.

'It's beautiful isn't it,' said David as he looked back, the strange factories in the distance, the different buildings and roads, James certain he could see his apartment somewhere in the distance.

James didn't know what to say, a little in shock that he was in-front of David Mitchell, the man most responsible for the misery he had been experiencing recently, and yet how the events had changed.

'It's alright,' said David.

'How much would you like?' said David, after a long pause.

'I'm sorry?'

'I said-   Look. Don't worry,' said David, 'I guess I would feel the same way if I was in your situation. Follow me.'

—

Whilst for the most part the introduction of Led into his owner's lives played out to be a success, unfortunately this didn't last as long as the family would have hoped for.

For Led did everything that was asked of him, performing all the jobs he was required to do and with great satisfaction from his owners. But it was ultimately due to his programming that led him to risk his own life and others around him, which resulted in the termination of his contract with his owners.

It happened on an evening downtown when Led's owners decided they would take a trip to the cinema to watch the latest family film release. It was a hot day during the summer holidays and the father was in want of a break from work and an evening out with the family, Led was invited. The film was a hit with the family, with even Led remarking how much he had enjoyed it.

It was when the family came out of the cinema that it happened, the strange and sudden sound of gunfire a few blocks down the road, people screaming and running for cover when the shots rang out. The family beckoned Led to come back into the cover of the cinema as people started ringing the police, a strange hubbub and heir of fear rising around the proximity. But it was like Led had something else on his mind that day. 'Someone could be in clear and present danger,' said Led quietly, 'A shot to the body could lead to fatality, I must help,' said Led as he looked at the family and then to the direction in which the shots rang out.

'No,' cried the father of the family as the two girls huddled together with their parents. 'I must help,' said Led bravely again.

Printed in Great Britain
by Amazon